HE IS MY FAIRYTALE

LILLIAN

To those who belive there is still place for true and pure love in this fake world.

Contents

Prologue

Three years ago I lost my parents and I was left alone and I lost my voice too. I built a barrier around my heart so that I can find a hope to live. But one day he came into my life and broke all those barriers I built. So, I dared give him broken pieces of heart believing that he'll fix it keep it safe.

FIRST MEET

Hrithik:

In the dark night at 10'o clock I'm going back to home after doing my part-time job. That's when I saw a person sitting at the lake under the full moon all alone with her back to me but I can feel her sadness. I don't why but I feel like she's going to break any time. In the middle of my thoughts suddenly I heard my phone is ringing sound so I check it to see who it is. It turns out my mom, so I attend the call then she asks "Hrithik where are you it's already 10 at night and you are still not home." Hearing that I said "mom I just finished my work I had to over time today and I'm going to come in an hour ok. Bye mom talk to you when I'm back". With that I cut the call at rise my head to see her that's when I saw her face under the moon light her face looks so delicate and beautiful. Her eyes are empty and cold. Then she turns her head and rise from the ground to stand and turns around to leave. I saw her walking far away. But just stand there looking at her back. After she disappeared into the night then I turn around to leave to go home.

By the time I reached home I saw my parents are waiting for me to have dinner together. When I saw them, I flashed them smile and they returned it to me. Then mom says "Hrithik take bath and come down then we can have dinner". I said OK and then returned to my room after 15min I came down and went to dining table where my parents are seated then mom asks "how is school and work"? "Everything is good mom" that's when dad says "why don't you just quit the job now your brother is also doing work in a best company with best salary so you just concentrate on your studies". When I heard what dad says I thought is best to quit job and concentrate on my studies with that I said "OK dad I'll going to stop my work from tomorrow" hearing that they both smiled at me and we start to talk about the other things suddenly I thought of her the girl who's lonely in the dark night.

When I'm thinking about her mom called me "Hrithik?" "Yes mom."

"Did something happened you seem to be spaced out". I said "no mom I'm alright just thinking about my college". When I said that suddenly dad said "Hrithik your brother called me saying that he wants you to change college and he already selected the best arts college for you if you want to join then you can enroll in it what do you say"? "Do as you all see it best Dad whatever your decision, I'll be ok with it". When dad heard that he smiles at me and the rest of the dinner they discussed about other things. After dinner I went to my room to sleep.

After a week later I get to join in my new arts college. Today is the first day for me in this college I don't know anyone here. When I checked my watch to see time, I say I saw that its already 9 so, then I hurriedly went inside the school to get to know my class. After getting know my class I went to class with class teacher. Good morning class today we have a new student, please come introduce yourself. Hello everyone I'm Hrithik it's a nice meeting you all hope we can be good friends. Ok Hrithik take the empty seat there. Yes mam. With that I went to take my seat. After that the morning classes went on peacefully.

During the lunch when I'm walking to see the campus, I suddenly saw figure sitting on the bench alone. Her back looked the similar. When I was thinking whether she's is the girl or not I saw another girl came and stood on her back and she patted on the girls shoulder. When she looked back I saw her face. It is the girl whom I saw that night. She is sitting alone like that night. Firstly, when I saw her, I was surprised in all of the place I never thought I would come to see her here. I'm happy that I can see her. I want to talk to her. When I'm contemplating whether to go talk to her or not then I saw the girl who came brought her lunch saying to her "Adhya eat this. You didn't eat anything since morning have it". When I heard her name Adhya it's such a nice name. She didn't take the food that the girl brought to her, the girl seems to know that she will refuse if so with a sigh she says "Adi please eat you are getting weak day by day so please Adi have some. Eat now".

I don't know why but she suddenly turned her face to back she looks where I'm standing when she saw me, she looked directly into my eyes saying. They are still the same like that night only filled with emptiness. Just like that day she turned her head towards her friend and took the food from her to eat. I know she recognized me the look in her eyes told that she recognized me. I went forward to talk to her when I'm standing beside her friend says; "Excuse me who are you"?

"Hi I'm Hrithik from arts group. And you are? I'm new here".

"Oh; hi I'm Nikitha and this is my friend Adhya and we are from literature. I'm sorry my friend doesn't like to talk with strangers please don't mind".

"No, it's alright. Hi Adhya I'm Hrithik". Saying that I put my hand forward to shake with her then her friend Nikitha told "Hrithik she won't like to" but then I feel a soft touch on my hand then I looked down only to see that Adhya is holding my hand, Nikitha said that "it was her first time she reacted to a stranger and hold the hand maybe she truly treats you as a friend except with me she never reacted to others". Then Adhya with draw her hand when she did it, I feel empty. Then I turned to her and smiled at her after looking at me for few seconds she lowered her head and starts to eat again. "Ok then Nikitha I need to leave class is going to start soon".

"Oh, Ok Hrithik meet you soon we are going back to home as we have no classes from now today".

Then I bent down and says" bye Adhya; take care see you again". She looked into my eyes and just nodded her head. Then I turned around and left.

Adhya:

When I'm waiting for my friend Nikitha who went to get lunch for us, I felt someone was staring at me and I felt the gaze was same because I felt same feeling last week in the park only to find a stranger staring at me because at that time most probably a few are on the road and there I'm standing at the edge of the lake in the late night. So, I turned around to look whether my guess is correct or not and there I saw him standing within few feet distance away from me even I didn't show any reaction on my face I was stunned for a moment to see him because I never thought that of all places I'm going to see here. Then I immediately turned my head only to find Nikitha walking to me with food in her hands and she gives it to me I didn't take the food because I have no appetite to eat anything she knows it but also she asked me again and this time I still felt the gaze on me so I turned my head to see who then I saw him my guess is right when I felt its familiar I thought of him but I never thought that it's really him the boy from that night. When I look into his eyes, I feels that he recognized, like I did but I didn't dare to entertain that thought. So, I turned my head and took the lunch from Nikitha to eat. I thought he would leave instead he walked towards us. When he held his hand out to shake with, I don't know why but I did it I shake my hand with him. After that when he bent down to say he is leaving I nodded my head but in reality, I don't want him to leave. It's just that when he smiles it feels warm. And I like it.

CHAPTER TWO

BIRTHDAY PARTY

Hrithik:

When I'm walking back to class I was thinking about Adhya and when she held my hand, I felt that it's so warm that and her hand is soft. Then I went to class and I sat in my seat and my desk mate start talking we become friends in no time his name is Jay when we are speaking my thought again travelled to the night that I first saw Adhya under the moon light she shines bright but her eyes are empty. While I'm thinking about that my thought are interrupted as when I feel that someone shaking me then I turned my head to see its jay. "Hey Hrithik are you ok. "Yes, I'm; why? "Oh, it's nothing it's just that you seem to lost in thoughts. "It's nothing I just thinking about something."

It's been two weeks since I joined in the college my friendship with Adhya has been improved a lot. What she doesn't know is that I have been learning hand signs. And she doesn't need to know about it. Thinking about Adhya and her small face and her smile unknowingly put my mind and heart on ease. When I was thinking about all these I was disturbed when Jay came and sat beside me and asked "What is your plans tonight?"

"My plans tonight it's Nothing'. 'Ok, then tonight is Kriti's birthday party she told me to ask you to attend".

"Alright I think I can attend, by the way at which time". Jay said "it's at 7 o'clock".

"Okay then meet you there".

Time flew without knowing it's already 6:30 and I just remembered that I need to attend Kriti's party. So, I got up and get dressed up in 15min's and left home telling my parents I'm attending my friend's party. By the time I reached there I saw some of my classmates who just arrived in them I saw Jay who just reached their and we both went inside her house with other classmates. Her house is three floor duplexes. After we settled down, Kriti's mother came and gave us some drinks and she said that Kriti will come down in few minutes. After she left us some of us are started playing games and some are talking how they decorated the house. After like it's 30 min's Kriti came down she dressed up beautifully but My eyes were on the girl next to her it's Adhya she's walking next to her even her face didn't show any of her emotions she looks beautiful in her sky-blue color lehenga which makes her look so delicate. She is too beautiful that I can't take my eyes of her. I never thought that Adhya will come to this party. When she came down with her friend Nikitha, they both walked over to the empty place and sat there. I saw that Adhya was nervous and held Nikitha's hand. And Nikitha is saying something to her to which she nods her head and seems to relax a bit. Then I made my way straight to them firstly I wished Nikitha and turned to Adhya when I greeted her, she just nods her head. "Hi Adhya".

Adhya:

When I sit on the sofa with Nikitha, I was too nervous because I know my aunt doesn't want me to come but it's my uncle who requested me, I want to decline the invitation but I can't because my uncle will be disappointed so I came I'm too nervous because I know my aunt will definitely use this chance to humiliate me. From last two years onwards that's when uncle health starts to deteriorate and aunt believes that it was because she always thought I'm a bad luck that's why my parents also died three years ago. When I came to their house after that my aunt totally disagreed with my uncle for allowing me to stay here. But because of uncle and Kriti she finally agreed. But she said to me that I need stay away from her daughter Kriti and uncle because she was afraid that something might happen to them because of me. Not only to me but she also warned saying that I'm bad luck whoever the person I'm close in my life they will not be happy. Even after what her mother said Kriti never left my side maybe not even until uncle suddenly fell ill. She always blames me for that and my aunt started to hate me. Thinking of all these made me more nervous. Feeling my nervousness Nikitha said "it's ok Adi I'm here for you maybe I think our aunt won't talk like that this time like how she always does think about it there are many are Kriti's classmates and they are also our friends right if she talks something badly not only will it affect you but also it will also destroy her daughter's birthday celebration, we know that she doesn't want her daughter to be sad so just relax we will leave as soon as possible". When I heard her words, I felt somewhat makes me feel relaxed.

After we sat there in silence, I felt someone is approaching us and it felt same presence so I raised my head to look and I saw Hrithik. When he greeted me, I just nodded my head and smiled at him. This two weeks with him are the happiest days. Even though he doesn't know or understand signs at first but now he can understand it easily. Just his presence alone keeps my mind in peace. And my heart will always welcome his warmth whenever he holds my hand.

While we three are talking we didn't notice how much time has passed. It was only until Kriti's mom called everyone saying that it's for cake cutting and we all went and she stood there in between everyone having a happy smile on her face and everyone is wishing her when I went near her to give her the gift her mom came and stood between us and saying that "you don't need to give her any gift just stay away from my daughter Adhya I don't want my daughter be in trouble". Those words made feel sad and I looked at Kriti only to find her hatred in her eyes and she turned her head. Since her father felt ill, they thought it was because of my fate which bring bad luck to the people around me. When I saw the look in her eyes, I felt like I can't stay their anymore so, placing the gift on the near table I left the place with Nikitha. When I went out, I heard Hrithik calling my name but I choose to ignore him and left the place.

CHAPTER THREE

HIS PROMISE

Adhya:

Time just flew by unknowingly it's been a week since the party. Since the party everything around me changed in class except Nikitha everyone started to avoid me like a plague and their comments are too harsh. The look in their eyes I know it too well because when my parents are dead and my relatives all saw me with the same look, I felt scared from the time I was born they all hate because they thought I'm sing of bad luck. But my parents and my brother will always cheer me up when I'm down because of their words and there was also Kriti with them she always been with me and played with me. We both used to go to school and music classes together. Every year on our birthday's we both used to play Villon together but from last three years I lost every one around me slowly. And I really started to believe that I'm really a bad luck. I want to know why they all thought like that about me. When my parents and brother died in that accident none of them came to me to say it's okay. Their death is a shocking news to me and I lost my voice from then due to shock they died in front of me but I can't do anything to save them to save me my brother pushed me out of the car and my parents and brother can't able to come out and the fire has started and I couldn't able to do anything just watching them burn alive in front of me like that I saw them just like that with my tears running down from my eyes I want to shouted for help but there was no one around me as it was past mid night I just sat there and cried until I lost my conscious by the time I woke up I was in hospital but there was no one with me. After discharging myself I went to home only to see all my relatives had left me alone. When I went in, I felt scarred and it's too lonely it always remembering me how my parents and brother left me alone. Maybe they did save me but they also left me alone. Remembering all these makes me too lonely. In this whole week I thought I can see Hrithik at least once but I didn't saw him maybe he too thinks same like others I don't blame him for that because firstly, I had no right to blame him because we are not even friends secondly, maybe it's true what others are saying about me, so I think it's best for him to stay away for me.

When I'm thinking all these, I felt a presence behind me and it's feeling is too familiar, I don't need to turn my head to know who because every time he's near I felt the same. Because no one has this positive vibe except him, he sat beside me on the bench and didn't say a word he just took my hand into his and we both sat there in silence. His hand is warm and it's giving a comfort feeling which I need after some time I heard Hrithik saying that "Adhya I'm sorry" and I was confused why he apologized me so I turned to look at him he seems to understand my confusion and he explained saying "that about the party after that day I want to come to you to see how are you doing but my brother came to home with his girlfriend to talk about their marriage and we all are busy with the preparations that's why I don't have any time now it's all set and I'm free, so don't think that I avoided because of those rumors ok and also remember that I'll never avoid you because of this stupid rumors."

When he said that I just nodded my head with my head down because I don't want him to see my tears, I just want to stop them but I can't because his words made me feel both happy and sad because it was the first time in these three years someone said that they don't want to avoid me. "Oh, by the way where is Nikitha you are sitting alone here. Didn't she come to college".

when he asked that I just nodded my head telling she didn't come today and he asked why then I told him with hand sign that *"she went to vacation with her family maybe she won't be back any time soon"*. "Alright then don't worry that you have me you don't have to be alone I be with you and accompany you until she comes when he said that I looked at him and asked in my hand sign *"so, it mean you won't be with me after she come"*.

When I asked him the he shook his head and laughed and said that "don't worry I'll be with you until you want me no not that even if you don't want me to be with you, I won't leave you" it's my promise. When I heard his words, I felt something different in my heart. And I just nodded my head for his with a small smile which came unknowingly. When he looked into at me directly into my eyes, I felt that his eyes are smiling looking into his eyes I felt that my heart beating fast. I just turned my head and looking at the lake Infront of me. After that we both just sat, there in silence. We both just their until it's getting dark, I didn't expect time goes too fast and then I heard Hrithik saying that "Adhya it's getting late come on let's go". After he stood up stretched his hand forward, I look at his stretched hand for few seconds and placed my hand on his then he held my hand and we walked out of the park.

When we reached out I left his hand and waved at him and turned to walk when I took few steps forward heard that Hrithik calling me so stopped and turned to look at him I saw him walking to my direction when he came he said that "It's already getting come on I'll walk with you up to your house then I'll leave", when I heard that I said that "it's not necessary my house just few streets aways from here and it's just 10mins to walk you go home I can go by myself" when he saw my signs he just shook his head and insisted on accompanying me. When I saw the stubborn look on his face I just sighed helplessly and nodded my head. We both walked in silence until we reached my home when we reached there, I signed him to come inside with my hands to that he just shook his head and said that next time he'll come saying that as it's getting dark, he needs to leave and then he bid a goodbye to me. I watched until he left and turned around to go inside when I opened the door the smile on my face has been faded the house felt too cold which made me shiver.

Sometimes this coldness left me feel lonely and scared out of my wits. For the first time in these three years, I felt this house is too cold and it makes me hard to breath I felt like I don't want to be here but slowly I made my way and went inside the house and stood in front of the photo that we took on my last birthday that I celebrated with them in which my brother kept his hand on my head and my parents were sitting in front of us. Then I went to my room took shower and came out of my room I just laid on the couch in hall looking at the photo in which we all are laughing thinking about that day makes me sadder because dad knows that on my birthday, I want to travel with them and celebrate it out not at our home. But my wish only made me lose everything thinking all these I closed my eyes and the tears are running down from my eyes without my knowledge.

Next day I woke up with my eyes swollen because of my crying last night. I look at the time it's 7 in the morning so I get up and walked to my room to get ready for my college after I got dressed up, I went to kitchen to prepare my breakfast. After having my breakfast, I took out my books to do my work which I didn't do last night. While I'm doing my work, I heard a knock on the door I was confused that who came this early normally no one will come to visit me I closed my books went to open the door to check who it is when I opened the I saw Hrithik standing there with a smile on his face it took me few minutes to react then I took him into the house when I went to kitchen and brought him water by the time I came out he settled himself after that I came and sat behind and asked *"why are you here at early morning?* Knowing my question, he said "You forget what I told you last night I said that I'll accompany you right so I came". When he said that I felt like tearing up thinking that even if he said I never thought he'll really be this serious. I'm so happy because he made me feel that I'm someone important to him but he doesn't need come this early in the morning *"You don't need to come it will be stressful to you moreover we can meet in college, right? "It's alright there's no trouble for me to come for you ok, never think you are a trouble for me"*.

When he said those words, I felt like my world has been starting to change. I felt like crying now but I don't want to do it in front of him so, turned my head in front to do my work. When I'm doing it, he suddenly asked that "Adhya can I call you with nick name how Nikitha calls you like Adi is it ok". When he asked that I nodded my head as approval. "Good than Adi why are you doing your work now". Hearing that I just said that *"It's just that last night I felt too lazy to do so I'm doing it now.* When he saw that he just nodded his head and he took out his book to read. By the time I finished my work it's already 8:30 I closed my books and Hrithik too got up and went out of the house after locking the door we started to walk to bus stop within 20mins we came to college.

CHAPTER FOUR

REALIZING THEIR FEELINGS

Hrithik:

As the both of us still had time for their classes, we just walked around the college. When the bell rang, Adhya said *"See you later"* and turned around and left. After that I also went to my class but I couldn't stop thinking about her swollen red eyes I saw when I went to her house this morning. I want to know what made her cry but I also know that even if I asked her, she won't tell me.

The one thing I knew about her mainly is that she needs time to get close to another person. Not because her trust was broken but only because she was scarred about what will happen to the person if she gets close. That day after she left, I thought that she needs time to get her emotions in control. So, I didn't go after her. The next day I called Nikitha and asked her what happened only then I get to know that her sudden lose of her parents and losing her voice but also facing the criticism from the people who are supposed to help her in her dark times. But all the choose to keep their hands aways by saying she was a bad luck which was utterly ridiculous. At such a young age she barred a lot of burned.

I know she wants time and I had so much time to give her. I'll never let any person talk back about her. After she lost her parents and brother, she doesn't have anyone but now she has me. I know that I'll never going to leave me.

That night when I saw her at the park, since then she occupied my every thought and just her thought makes my heart flutter. At first, I thought it was just an attraction but as the time passes, I knew that it was not an attraction it's more than that. Because if it's just an attraction I won't be thinking of keeping her in my life forever.

When saw jay who is sitting beside me, I thought for a second and asked him "Hey jay I need to ask you a question".

"What? you sounded like it's serious ask it"

"When you see a person and like her company and also wanted to spend more time with her to make her comfortable around you and also you wanted to spend you whole time with her what do you call that feeling?' Hearing my question, he looked at me and said "First of all you know that you want spend your whole with her then why are asking this"? "Just tell me" "then it is love. Hrithik listen to me you already know that you wanted to share your life with her so it means that you had feelings for her and you are in love with her". "Love" I murmured the word myself and thought 'maybe really I think I'm in love with Adhya'. When I thought that the thought it self is enough to make me happy. All I need is to wait until Adhya starts to open up to me. I can wait as much as time she needs. Because I know that I'm never going to leave her. Adhya will only be mine forever.

Adhya:

I can't able to concentrate on any class from morning. Whenever I try to concentrate my mind immediately drifted to the words Hrithik has said. After the end of the college Hrithik came with me to my house when I ask him, I can go on my own he only said "I like to do this Adhi you are never a trouble to me so don't think that and also I can't be in peace until I saw go inside the house with my own eyes". I just nodded my head and went inside after knowing that I'm safe inside he left from there.

After he left all, I could think about is his words and also when he came to my house at morning, he made me special. His smile and whenever he looks at me there is a concern in his gaze. Sometimes he made me feel like I'm someone important to him. With a smile on my face, I looked into mirror in my room my only thought is 'It's been a long since I smiled like this'.

Thinking I took out my dairy which I never thought I had another chance to use after I lost my parents and my brother. Turning every page and reading it only makes me want to cry because all the things I wrote in this dairy are all happy moments. Until they left me alone by all myself there is never a sad day in my life because mom and dad never let me had a hard day my life and my brother if he knew I want something he's the first person to give it to me. That's why I never took this dairy out after I lost them because I don't want to add any of my sad memories in this dairy.

But today I took it out but thinking about Hrithik but I don't know what to write in it. After 3year he's the reason for my smile and he's the reason to take it out. Thinking I opened the dairy and started to write

> *""It has been only 4weeks since the first time I saw him but he occupies a part of me which has been empty since I lost my parents and brother. All this I felt was lonely even Nikitha is with all the time and her parents also trying to be there for me I only felt lonely.*
>
> *But ever since Hrithik came into my life, I slowly started to feel that the gap in my heart is filling. Whenever we are together, he always holds my hand. The smile on his face whenever he looks at me makes me feel warmth. And I know that only he can make me feel like that no one else.*
>
> *But for sure I know one thing that "He's my safe place and he's my comfort place. The first time I saw in the park I saw the spark in his eyes which is real. That day after I returned home, I can't stop thinking about him.*
>
> *But after one week later when I saw him in college, I was really shocked I thought he won't recognize my but what I didn't expect was that not only did he recognized*

me but also, he initiated to talk with me.

And also, after Kriti's birthday everyone started to avoid me but he never avoids me and said that he'll never leave me. When I heard those, I thought he was just saying to make me feel better but now I understood that he didn't say those words to make feel good but he only said that because he means it. Whenever I thought about it, I always feel something different in my heart. And whenever I left his hand before we go into the class or after dropping at my house, I only want to hold it longer because whenever he's with me I feels like this world isn't as cold as it actually feels.

But I know that whatever I'm feeling towards Hrithik is not a simple attraction it's something more than that and I know what is it but I don't to say the name because I had a feeling that if I start to understand and name whatever I'm felling now something are going to change but I don't know whether they are good or bad changes. So, I won't name it or try to understand it because I like this confusion"."

After writing it I closed my dairy and lay down on the bed and closed my eyes. After sometime I heard my phone ringtone which shows me that I got a message 'Who will text me and that to at this time'. Thinking that I opened my phone only to see the text from Hrithik only to find him asking

Hrithik: "Adhi did you finished your dinner?"

Me: "Just now I finished. What about you"?

Hrithik: "Still no."

Hrithik: "Adhi tomorrow it's holiday right so do you want to come out with me".

Seeing that I don't know how to answer his question. The thought of spending time with him alone makes me nervous. But I too excited.

Me: "Yes"

Hrithik: "Ok then I'll come to pick you up in the morning".

Me: "Alright"

Hrithik: "Good night, Adhi sleep well"

Me: "Good night".

After that I put my phone aside and started to think about where he will take me tomorrow. After 5minutes as I felt so sleepy so I turned off the bed light and dozed off.

Hrithik:

When I saw her room lights are turned off, I knew that she slept and she was safe. From the first day I met Adhya at school from then on, I always follow her until I know she safely reached home. Even Nikitha accompanies her every day and somedays she spent her night at Adhya's home I can't help but worry about her. She doesn't need to know about that and she won't because all these days I only waited outside her house and left only after knowing that the lights in her room have been turned off and she slept safely. Looking at the time as it was already past nine, I knew that mom and dad and also my brother will be waiting for me at home for dinner. So, I turned around and left to my home.

By the time I came back I saw mom and dad are sitting in the living room. When they saw me, mom came towards me with a smile and told me take bath. After taking my bath I came to dinning only to find my brother also joined.

After dinner I left to my room because my parents are going to discuss about my brother's marriage. Laying on the bed I took my phone unlocking it I opened the photos of Adhya which I had taken when she was not looking.

When I was looking at the photos, I heard the knock on my followed with mom's voice "Hrithik I'm coming".

"Mom come sit why are you here aren't you all talking about my brother's marriage". "Nothing I just saw you were looking absent minded these days. Did something happen"?

"No mom everything is good it's just I'm thinking about my classes".

"Alright then but remember that if you had any problem or anything to discuss we are here for you always."

"I understood mom just don't worry I'm good mom". "Ok then it's getting late sleep now Good night". "Good night mom".

After my mom left the room, I again started to think about Adhya and her reaction to the surprise when take her to the place I planned.

Adhya:

Next morning, I wake up early than other day because I can't able to stop thinking about Hrithik he said he will take out today. In these three I never went to anyplace even when my friends are going because I'll miss my brother even more. In past every time we go on a trip he'll never allow to go away from his sight. And he'll always hold my hand because he feared that I'll go missing. But after he left all alone, I never went out with anyone because now my brother won't be with me to hold my hand and to take care of me. And also, the thought of him not being there for me left me sacred. But today I dared to go out not just because anyone but only because Hrithik.

By the time Hrithik came it was already ten. "Good morning, Adhi did you sleep well last night". When he asked that I nodded my head and asked with my hands *"Morning What about you did you sleep well"?*

He saw what I'm asking he smiled and said "Yes I slept well". "So, now are you ready to go out". Hearing his question, I nodded my head eagerly seeing that his smile widened. And we both went out after locking the door he said "Adhi first we'll have something to eat and we'll go ok".

When he said that I nodded my head. Seeing that I agree to his suggestion he took my hand and held it. When I looked at our intertwined hands where his big hand is fully covering my small hand in his as if he's protecting it. Then I looked at up at him I can only see his back because he's walking in front of me by holding my hand as if he's protecting me from every problem in front of me. Looking at him like that I know that he's my safe place. When I looked at our shadows both of our shadows are combined with each other as it is one person when I saw that I smiled and looked back at him.

He took me to a restaurant to have some breakfast. After that he said he wanted take me to watch a movie in theater. When he said that I thought 'it's really been a long time since came out to watch a movie. Three years it's particularly long time.' So, when Hrithik said that I didn't answer to him immediately so turned to look at me and said "Adhi if you don't want to go then we won't ok all I need for you is feel comfortable".

Hearing that I know what he's trying to do he wants me to feel comfortable around him. But what he doesn't know is that not only I'm comfortable and free when I'm with him also I feel safe and also if he's by my side I can face this world and whatever the criticism it sent to me because I know that he'll be my support. So, I looked at him and nodded my head as and understanding and said *"I had no problem to watch movie I'll be comfortable as long as you will be my side"*. He looked at me with his eyes filled with smile and looking gentle he held on to my hand and led me to the ticket counter and said that "You stay here there is a lot of crowed so I'll go and get tickets for us". When said that I nodded my head and he left to get tickets for us. After few minutes he came out of the crowed and tickets and his hands filled with popcorn and drink. So, I went near him and took the drinks from his hand so that he can hold popcorn freely. After we went into the cinema hall after I saw the title of the movie only then I understood that it was both romantic and comedy movie. As the movie is two and half hour's duration by the time, we came out it was nearly two in the afternoon. And I'm also started to feet little hungry. With in 15minutes he takes me to a nearby restaurant. After sitting at the table nearby a window. Hrithik ordered most of my favorite when I heard that I asked him *"why do you ordered all my favorite just order something you like too"*. When he saw my hand signs, he immediately what I'm saying and said "I can eat anything so it's not a problem".

By the time we completed our lunch it was already Three thirty during the whole time he said about his family and when I asked him about his brother's marriage, he told me how they are preparing everything and how his brother was so happy that he participated in everything and how he selected according to his girlfriend likings. After that he took me to the beach when we went there, I said his I don't want to takes of my heels. The only reason is that since my childhood my brother always let me walk on his feet so that my foot gets hurt. And my father to sometime copies my brother by let our mom walk on his feet.

When he saw that he let me shit on the bench and he sat on is one knee in front of me and took my shoes I was shocked and can't able to react. When he did that, I want to stop him but before I can say a word, he went back on his feet and held out his hind and said "Believe me Adhi just come with me". When he said that I put my hand in his and stood up the he said "Put your feet on mine". When I heard that I looked at him with a wide eye because I never thought that he can let he walk on his feet. When I looked at him, he just said "Do it Adhi just believe in me". When I heard that I put my feet on his and then he walked us both towards the water. When the wave hit us, he pulled me into him as he held me so carefully. When the water touched our feet the coolness of the water made my fast-beating heart and nervousness calmed down a bit. The warmth from his body made me feel safe. When I looked up to look at him I felt I was so small in front of him because I only up to his chest and when I looked at him as the sun was setting the rays falling on him his face looks so ethereal maybe there won't be any man who can look go gentle like him. I don't know what happened to me at that moment I just wanted to hear his heartbeat so, I leaned my head and put in on his chest and wrap my hands around him and closed my eyes. I felt that he also putting his hands around me safely and pulled me closer to me. When heard his steady heartbeat, hearing it made me comfortable and we stood there like that for God knows how much time.

CHAPTER FIVE

SURPRISE

Adhya:

After sometime I heard Hrithik asking me "Adhi is what you said in the morning is true"? When I heard that I didn't understand about what he's asking so looked at with. When understood the confusion on my face he said "That you said you are comfortable with me is it true". Hearing that I understood what it is so I just nodded my head. Seeing that his eyes lit up the smile in his eyes felt like a *"The light comes after the dark rainy day"* and put his hand on my cheek and stroked it gently with his thumb while looking into my eyes. This moment felt so real and all I want is to capture this moment. And also, all want is to stop the time so that I can have this moment for long. After sometime he took me to nearby bench to sit and he left. After few minutes he came back with ice creams in his hand when I looked at him there is a gentle smile on his face as he carefully handover me the ice cream. He brought my favorite straw berry flavor. After that he sat besides, we both sit there in silence watching the sun set. The silence between us isn't awkward but it strangely feels comfortable and I don't want to disturb. Maybe I think he feels the same to that's why he didn't take any initiative to talk. While I'm watching the sun set, I sometimes feel him staring at me. But I didn't turn and only continued to watch sun set.

By the time we left from there it was already dark I thought we are going home but he said "Not now Adhi there is still time and I want to show you something else also". After he said that he takes to the park where we first saw each other when we came here, I looked at his and asked with my hands *"Why did you brought me here"?* When he understands what I'm asking he said "just wait for some more time". After saying that we both sat there under a tree. After sometime Hrithik said "Adhya do you want to know why I brought you hear"? When I heard his question, I nodded my head saying yes. Seeing that he stood up and stretched his hand to me when I took his hand, he helped me stand up and took me near the lake when I stood there, I felt a sudden darkness only to find that Hrithik closed my eyes with his hand. My stood behind and put his chin on my shoulder and said *"HAPPY BRITHDAY ADHYA"* saying that he took his hand and I opened my eyes on to find the so many fireflies are flying around us by producing a greenish yellow light. Only then I realized that today is my birthday. After three years I didn't cry on this day.

After my parent's death I marked this day as a black day. But today Hrithik made this day colorful. He is like a light to my darkness. Now he stood by my side while holding my hand. Thinking about every thing from the morning my eyes teared up when I looked at him, he said "Today is not the you should cry Adhya you have to smile". When I heard that I just nodded my head but I can't stop tears. But then I suddenly heard a familiar voice "Why are you still crying girl"? When I heard that I turned only to find Nikitha is standing there with the cake in her hands and there is a wide smile on her face I also saw her parents behind her and they were also smiling with her. Not only them but I also saw some others whom I don't know so I turned to Hrithik "They are my parents and my brother". Only then I understood he brought his parents to. Then Nikitha came near to me with cake and said "Happy birthday Adhi now cut the cake". After that she put cake in Hrithik's hand and light up the candles on the cake. After that Hrithik said blow the candles and make a with. Saying that he put the cake in front of me. Then I closed my eyes and wished "I want to be with Hrithik forever and I want him to be safe". Wishing that I opened my eyes and blown the candles. After cutting the cake I gave it first to Hrithik. When Nikitha saw that she said "Girl now you are forgetting you best friend huh". When I heard that I smiled and cut the big piece to give her after both Nikitha's and Hrithik's came and wished me. And I thanked them by showing the hand sign.

After Hrithik's parents invited us all to their house for dinner. During dinner the whole time she sat beside me and talked about so many things and we both laughed a lot and sometimes Nikitha and her parents also joined with us. At that moment it felt so warm like a home and eyes watered unknowingly. So, I immediately turned my face so that no one can see those. Then I turned to see Hrithik only to find him already staring with a smile when he saw that I'm looking at his he smile widened and he asked "Do like the surprise Adhi"? When I heard his question, I nodded my head with a smile. The moment I wished that I want to be with him forever at that moment I can't deny it anymore even when if I don't want to name it in all these days now I can't help but it because only he made me feel it because "I love him and 'He's is my Fairy tale'. In which he is my prince."

After dinner Hrithik's mom took me to garden as we both walked out, we sat on the chair in the garden and she held my hand and said "Never think that you are alone in this world Adhya from this moment onwards we are all there for you". When she said those, I can't stop my tears anymore so, I let them out and went near her and sat down on the ground and put my head in her lap and hugged her waist. Maybe I think she understood my feelings so she just put her hand on my head and said "It's alright let it out totally only then you can be free. And then everything is going to be fine". Hearing those words, I cried even more because no said to me those words. All these years I'm waiting for someone who can tell me those words but no one said that and left me all alone. After some time, I calmed down and just there like that and she put her hand on my head and patted it feels warm like because mom always put her hand on head and pat it slowly and gently for me to sleep. When Hrithik's mother is doing that, I felt the same and closed my eyes and fell asleep.

Hrithik:

When I took Adhya out this morning, she doesn't have a single clue what I planned for her. Nikitha once told me that she didn't celebrate her birthday for last three years because she lost her parents and brother on that day. I always want Adhya to be comfortable around me but she said that she is I felt happy. I want her to forget about the darkness of this day so I took her to a movie after that when we went to, she said she doesn't want take of her heels I just let her to stand on my feet during that time she was very close to me. But she wrapped her hands around and put her head on my chest with a small smile on her face at that moment I only know one thing I'll do anything if it makes smile like that every day. And when she watched the fireflies in the park, she looked at me like I'm her world and she's ready to keep it in my hands.

After dinner mom took Adhya out for a walk to the garden where we all can see them. But due to some reason she suddenly hugged mom and started to cry by seeing that I stood up and to and ask her but when I'm about to take a step I heard Nikitha's mother saying "Don't go now she needs to let it out because she buried so many things inside her heart and closed it so that no one can see that. Just let her maybe only than she can free". When I heard that I took a step back and looked outside. Nikitha who saw that also started to cry. Then I felt a hand on my shoulder on to see my father and my brother are standing beside me. And then I heard my father saying that "Sometimes it takes time to make everything better remember one thing Hrithik you are going to be the reason for her smile in the future but also remember that she dared to shed everything and dared to see light because of you so don't make her see the darkness again because if she has to face it again maybe she can't able to come out of it next time". When I heard what da said I understood the meaning of his words so I nodded my head and continued to look out only to see her slept in mom's lap. Seeing I understood dad just patted my back and left my brother told me to be careful and left from there.

Then I went out and said to mom that I'm going to take her inside. Hearing that she nodded her head and let me take her. So, I bent down a took her in my arms and take her to my room and covered with a blanket seeing her red nose because of crying I felt a stab in my heart then I leaned forward and pressed my lips on her forehead. After I turned around only to find mom near the door with a smile on her face. I know what she's going to ask me so I left the room and gently closed the door. When I went down to the leaving room, I saw that Nikitha and her parents are ready to leave. But when her mother saw me, she came towards he and held my and said "After so many this is the first, I saw her smile on this day thank you so much take care of her never make her cry again". When he said that I understand why she told me those words so I nodded to her and said "I'm never going to make her cry again". When I assured her, she around to leave then I saw her husband looking at me with a smile and said "Take care of her she faced a lot". With that they both left the house. Then Nikitha said "Thank you so much Hrithik". After saying that she too left the house while mom went to send them of.

After sending them of she came inside sitting beside me mom let out a small smile and said "So, she is the girl who made my son act absent minded and also smile like a stupid with out reason". When I heard what mom said I knew that she can understand that I love Adhya so, I didn't it and said "Yes mom do you like her"? When she heard that she looked at me and said that "Even if I say I don't like her with your personality I know you won't leave her just because what I said". When I heard that I just let out a small laugh "Mom you know your son too well". "Don't worry I love her but remember one thing Hrithik Don't ever make her cry again not because of anyone or you. Mainly you don't become the reason for her darkness again because now you are the reason, she dared to crush all her wall she built around her heart so that she can continue to live. If she again built those because of you maybe there won't be next for her. For her you are the most important person to her. Because when everyone around he saw her as a curse but you are only person who saw her as a human but not a curse. Maybe that's the reason she dared to hold your hand. So, never leave her hand Hrithik. Her heart is very delicate if you leave her, she can't able to bare it because this time she kept all her broken pieces in your hands because she believes that only you can arrange it and keep it safe. So, keep it safe Hrithik and don't miss any piece". When I heard what mom said I know that she understands her and nodded her head. "Mom if anything were happened to me do you also see her like a curse than". "Hrithik all these nonsense like curse and all are believed by people who feared for their lives and those with lack of knowledge and moral because to cover their flaws, they use it but there is nothing like that. If something were to happen to you, I only believe that its fate because whatever written in it no one can change it. Now it's getting late sleep good night". "Alright good night mom". After that she stood up and kissed on my forehead and left.

It's been two weeks since that day from then onwards I can see that Adhya is smiling more and more and it's her real smile and it is very beautiful. Today after both Nikitha and Adhya went to their class. After that I started to walk towards my classroom when I'm near the class I saw Kriti standing their when she saw me, she called me so I turned to her "Hrithik I need to talk to you about something please". When she said that I just nodded my head and then we went to the ground. When we sat there, she said "Hrithik I saw that Adhya is smiling a lot these days and I know that this was because of you so all I want to thank you first about it". When I heard what she said I'm shocked because still today I never thought that she cared about her because she never seems care about her. So, when I looked at her, she said "I know that what I said is shocking because you all think I hate her but that's not true. When I came to know that my father became ill and it was serious I can't able to take it that my father is going to leave me so I only blamed it on her to make me feel myself better but I also know that what I did is wrong blaming her for this is my mistake because when I'm the who should need to be by her side during her bad days but I choose to blame her and left all alone by herself. I also I hurt her but at the same time I started to hurt myself too because to me she's not only my cousin but she is also my best friend and my dairy with whom I can share everything. I only want to say one thing to you Hrithik I saw her smile the real one not the fake after three years and I know that you are the reason for it. And I appreciate that because when everyone around her abandoned her only you went near her gave her the courage for her to smile. So please don't ever let her loose it because this time it's you who showed her the light so keep her safe. Maybe by now you can understand her that she is very sensitive she never let others to see her sadness she only bares it by herself to make her stronger but what she doesn't know is that she can't bare it forever. That's why I'm asking you to be there for her if she's feeling down. And also, if I ever get to know that you made broken, I'm will be the person to whom you should need answer and I won't forgive you." When heard that I said "you don't have to worry about it I'll take care of her". After that Kriti left from there. I was shocked by her words because never have I thought that Kriti will warn be because of Adhya but when I think back what she said I understood that Adhya is very important person to her.

CHAPTER SIX

ACCIDENT

Hrithik:

After that I returned to the class. After the classes are completed, I picked my bag and went to Adhya's class today Jay also accompanied me to come I told him about how I feel about Adhya and he said that "if she likes you in return than I can say that you are lucky so don't miss her". Hearing is answer I smiled. By the time we reached to her class we saw both Adhya and Nikitha are standing outside the classroom with their bags. When they saw us, they smiled and I went to Adhya taking her bag with one hand and with my free hand I held her hand. When Jay saw this, he looked at me meaningfully and said "You need to give me all the details Hrithik". When he said that I smiled and said "it's getting late so we should need leave come on". Saying that I led Adhya outside and both Nikitha and Jay follow behind us. Tonight, we all plan stay at Adhya house from last week most of the days both me and Nikitha stayed at her home. So, when we are walking to her house, I saw the flower bouquet shop which is at the opposite side of the school when I saw it, I said to Adhya and my friends to "wait for me here and I'll be quick" saying that I crossed the road and I tell the lady to make bouquet with rose and Lily. Within few minutes the lady prepared the bouquet and gave it to me while I'm paying my bill she said "is it for your girlfriend"? "No, she still not my girlfriend but she's going to be in near future". When I said that the lady smiled and took out a card and write something in it and attached it to bouquet. When I see the card, I smiled because it says "I'll be with you forever". When see that I thanked the lady and she said "Best of luck". After that I left the stop but at one moment I was standing and the next moment I'm lying on the ground with blood and I feel like I can't able to move my body at that I heard a voice shouting my name "HRITHIK" only then I saw her running towards me when she came and sat on the road and calling my name I smiled because her voice it's sweet and melodious. Not only that the word she spoke after all these years is my name. Then felt my conscious is slowly slipping away and darkness is slowly coming to me. The last moment before I totally am Adhya holding me and crying while calling my name.

Kriti:

After I talked with Hrithik I was more at ease because now I know there is someone who will hold her hand and help her stand up when she fell down. After classes I returned home early because mom said that my elder uncle his family and my grandparents are coming home. When I went inside, I saw them all talking with each other when mom saw me told me sit beside her. Just as I'm about sit my phone rang when I saw it is Nikitha, I immediately attend the call only to hear saying "Kriti come to general hospital fast Adhya she" when I heard Adhya name I was panicked and asked "What happened to Adhi why are you in hospital"? "Adhi is good but Hrithik he got into an accident and we rushed him to the hospital still then onwards she didn't talk or cried she is sitting here in silence I'm feeling scared please come fast". When I heard that it was Hrithik we got into an accident I know that it's going to be a huge blow on her and if something happens, she won't able become normal again. When I thought that the itself made me scared because I know if something goes wrong, I'm going to lose my best friend forever no it can't be happened so I turned around and ran outside I didn't even bother to wait and explain to my parents and my relatives because now Adhi is most important.

I immediately asked our driver to take me to general hospital as fast as possible. Within 20 minutes I arrived at hospital and ran to

Hrithik's ward only to find Adhya sitting there still in her uniform like a statue but I can see that her hands are trembling I also saw an elder lady sitting beside her and hold Adhya's hand I know that she can't take it anymore because I saw her like this on that day three years ago when none of our family members went near her. That when I get to know that she discharged from hospital so went to her house only to find her laying down on the cold ground she was trembling a lot but it's not because of the cold but because she was alone and she don't know how to express. When I went to, I found that at that she lost her voice and it was because of psychological trauma. Now seeing her like this only made me more scared so I ran towards and I sat on my knees and hugged her and said "he'll be OK Adhi so don't worry everything will be ok". When I said that I heard her calling my name "Kriti" when I heard that I'm shocked because she didn't talk to anyone all these but now listening her calling made me crying because she had this sweet gentle voice, I missed hearing it now again I heard her calling me. Then again, she said "Please tell him to wake up Kriti I can't able bare this if I lost him there won't be any meaning to my life, please I can't able to live without him". When I heard that I know that his accident will be a big throne in her heart but when I heard that I knew that she won't be able to live if something happens to him. When I saw the operation is still going on I said "Adhi doctors are still operating on him so all we need to do is wait here don't lose hope nothing will happen to him he'll be fine believe me he'll be out of danger". When I said that I saw a small hope in her eyes and she said "Really is that true" when I heard that I nodded my head. But then I heard the elder lady voice who is sitting beside her saying "Adhya what she said is true he'll be fine you don't know that my son is too stubborn nothing can win under his stubbornness so relax a little dear". Only then I understood that she is Hrithik's mother. Hearing her words, I felt that her body relaxed a little and she stopped herself from trembling.

Just as I stood up, I saw my parents and our elder uncle and aunt are coming towards us seeing them I know that they both came here just to criticize her. Even before I can speak our aunt said "Adhya how many times we have to tell you not to cause trouble for anyone. Look there aren't you satisfied how because of you your parents and brother are dead and now look just because of you there is another life laying inside and fighting for life you are just a curse and bad luck why don't you simply just die so others won't be affected". When I heard her words, I can't able to take it anymore so I shouted at her "that's enough auntie you crossed the line today" no sooner I finished my words I heard a slap sound outside the ward and everything fell into a deep silence. When I saw my aunt holding her cheek, she looked at Hrithik's mom with a shocked expression and both my parents and my uncle also had same expression as my aunt but I felt delight because someone needs to show her what's her place.

Just as she was about to open her mouth, I heard Hrithik's mother angry voice as she said "shut up if you dare to speak you don't like what I'll do. Listen here the one inside is my son and the one you are cursing she is my son's girl it means she's the future daughter in law of my family. Even I didn't blame her for what happened then who are you to blame and tell her to die. And remember this from this moment onwards she had nothing to do with your family you maybe a relative of her but I don't care Adhya is my family and I don't like it when an outsider judges my family member. If you all see her as a curse then leave her because even if you all left her she'll never be alone because she has my family and we'll never leave her".

When I heard what she said I was shocked not only me but also Nikitha and Jay to. Then I thought "wait what she just said her future daughter in law " when I thought of it, I turned to Adhya only see her as shocked as me. But when I heard how she supported I don't have anything to worry about her from now on. And then we all just sat there in silence after sometime doctors who are in operation room came out then I saw Hrithik mom stood up but she didn't leave Adhya hand. Standing up she asked "Doctor how is my son"? "Nothing to worry he's out of danger and after two hours he will come into conscious then you can go and see him when Adhya heard doctor's words, I felt that she is totally relaxed. And murmured to herself "he's fine" "yes, he's Adhi now goes and wash your face you have to eat something". When I said that she shook her head and said "No I don't want to eat any thing I want to see him first". When I heard that I know that I can't force her so I just sat beside her.

Adhya:

When I saw Hrithik was hit by a car and his head was bleeding I was just scared at that time I don't even realize I got my voice back. At that time, I'm scared that he'll also leave me like how my parents and brother left me. He's my light is he also leaves me I don't know how I'm going to live with fact that he is not there by my side to walk with me and hold my hand. I don't know how we came to hospital because my mind couldn't able to process anything after how I saw Hrithik in blood. When I we arrived the hospital both Jay and Nikitha are with me when Hrithik is taken into ER I'm just standing there I can't even able to think anything even I can't able to process what Jay and Nikith's are talking.

Then I saw both Hrithik's parents and his brother are coming maybe at that time even if she blames me like all as sign of bad luck, I'll accept everything whatever his mother is saying. But the next moment she stood in front of me and hugged saying "Everything will be alright Adhi try to be brave". When I heard that I can't able to stop myself from crying so I let my tears leave while crying I said "Auntie Hrithik he's still in there I don't know how to be brave auntie after seeing him like that. Please tell him not to leave me like them I can't able to live auntie if something happened to him". When I said that she patted my back and made to look at her saying "Adhi he'll come don't worry look at me Adhi, he won't leave us because he still didn't hear your voice, he once told me that he'll do anything to make your voice come back again because he wants you to call his name so don't worry". Saying that she led me to the sit on the chair beside us and she sat beside me holding my hand both her husband and brother including Jay and Nikitha are all standing beside us.

It's been sometime but no doctors came out and I can't able to stop the trembling of my hands while I can't stop it, I felt someone hugging me and then I heard Kriti voice she said "he'll be OK Adhi so don't worry everything will be ok" just like three years ago when everyone left me alone in my home when I don't want to be alone than also it was Kriti who came for me and she stayed with even if her mother objected she stayed with me. When I again heard her voice, I can't able to control myself so cried out and said "Please tell him to wake up Kriti I can't able bare this if I lost him there won't be any meaning to my life, please I can't able to live without him". When she heard that she said "Adhi doctors are still operating on him so all we need to do is wait here don't lose hope nothing will happen to him he'll be fine believe me he'll be out of danger". Her words helped me to relax a little.

Just then I heard my elder aunt saying "Adhya how many times we have to tell you not to cause trouble for anyone. Look there aren't you satisfied how because of you your parents and brother are dead and now look just because of you there is another life laying inside and fighting for life you are just a curse and bad luck why don't you simply just die so others won't be affected". When I heard those words, I can't able to take it then I heard Krithi shouted on aunt but what I didn't expect is that Hrithik's mother to slap her she also said that I'm her future daughter-in-law when heard it I was shocked. When she came to hospital not only, she didn't blame me but now she is standing up for me by saying that I'm her family and they all will be with me. After sometime when the doctor came and said that he'll be fine only then I let myself to be relaxed.

Hrithik:

When I opened my eyes all I saw is the white ceiling and I feel the whole body is aching a lot only the I remembered that I had an accident and I heard her voice. Adhya's first word after three years is my name thinking about this, I can't help but smile then I heard "Mom I think Hrithik became mentally unstable". When heard that I saw my brother and my parents are standing by the door while mom is holding Adhya's hand. When I heard my brother's words I said "And what makes you think that"? "Oh, it's just you just woke up and you head has that bandage but you are still smiling like you are not in any pain that's why I thought that may be the accident did something to your brain". "Bro remembers this is I became like that then you have to be careful I can use it to torture you". When I said that all them laughed and mom came near me, I thought she'll ask about how I'm feeling but she raised her hand and slapped me on my shoulder as hard as she can. But I didn't say anything I know she is angry on me because I'm careful enough and got myself into and accident and I know she was scared just as mom about to open her mouth to start her lecture to me dad said "Come on let's go out you can talk to him later give them both some time alone". Saying that he led my mom out side and my brother followed behind them leaving me and Adhya alone

"Hrithik" when I heard her calling my name, I can't help but say "Say it again Adhi". "Hrithik" when she said again, I took her hand pulled her to me and hugged her "Your voice is beautiful Adhi say my name once again". "Hrithik" when she said that again her voice this time became even gentle and I heard her crying when I'm about to pull her to see her she wrapped her hands around my neck and said "I'm so scared Hrithik when I saw you in blood, I thought you'll also leave me like them. I can't be able to live if you leave me Hrithik". While she is saying that she chocked on her words in middle because she is crying hard. When I heard her words, I can't help but tighten by hold around her and said "I won't leave you Adhi I promise I'll never ever let you be alone in this world again princess". When she heard that she held more tightly and clung to me as if she was scared to let go of me if she did maybe she won't able to held me again. After few minutes I pulled her away from me and I looked at her. Her eyes are red and swollen and the tip of the nose changed into red shade.

I leaned forward and held her small face in my hands and put my forehead on hers and said in a low voice "I'll be with you forever princess it's my promise" when I said that she closed her eyes and smiled a little.

Time passed it's been a month since I got into accident before I get discharged doctor said that I need a month bed rest after that everything will be ok. After that day Adhya came to my home everyday to take care of me my parents also didn't object her. Now she's talking a lot and her voice is so sweet and I like to hear it forever. And also, she's starting to learn cooking from my mother. Now she either stays at my home or stay at Kriti's home after Kriti said sorry to her and explained why she left her Adhya didn't say anything to her she was just happy that Kriti and her family accepts her again. Today I planned a surprise for her so I asked both Nikitha and Kriti to the park where we saw each other for the first time.

CHAPTER SEVEN

CONFESSION

Adhya:

These are the happiest days in my life. Because I got my best friend back and aunt also changed how she used to be with me three years ago. Now that we Me, Kriti and Nikitha are hanging out together like how we used to do it in past. Most of the I spend my time with Hrithik by taking care of him. And also, I started to learn cooking from his mother. She's very patient with me. I felt like I'm with mom whenever I'm with her.

Now I'm came to park with both Kriti and Nikitha this place always makes me feel peaceful. When we are sitting near the lake, we talked about many things like how we used to take ice cream without our parents notice and after find out how we said it on my brother so that we can escape from our mother's scoldings. These days whenever I think about my parents and brother I didn't feel as heavy as it felt before but I always wished that if they were here at this moment maybe it will be more beautiful.

While we are talking the lights around the park are turned off so I said "hey what happened why the lights are gone"? When I said I didn't receive any answer from both Kriti and Nikitha so turned my phone flash on to find the spots where they are sitting is empty. So, I stand up and called their names "Kriti, Nikitha where are you both"? When didn't receive the answer, I thought to call them but then I saw the lights on in a straight way on both the sides and the rose petals are covered the whole path while I was thinking who did it, I got a message on my phone from Hrithik saying "Follow the light princess". When I saw the message, I understood he is the one who did this. But whenever he calls me princess my heart trembles.

After see that I followed the path only to find myself in a heart shaped symbol which is made with roses and light are around it. Then the lights around are come back and is the words "*MARRY ME*" Seeing that I can't able to stop my tears this time they are coming because of my happiness. Then I turned around only to find Hrithik is standing before me with a rose bouquet in his hand then he smiled at me at sat on his one knee and said "Adhi will you marry me and let me hold your hand forever". Saying that he took out small velvet color box and opened it and put it in front of me only to find a ring in it. Seeing it I'm to stunned to answer then when I heard a familiar voice and when I looked around, I find both Kriti and Nikitha with their parents and also Jay and finally I saw Hrithik's parents and brother who came with his future wife. I heard all of them saying "Say yes". Then I turned to see Hrithik and saw him smiling at me his eyes are bright then I took the bouquet from him and nodded my head and said "Yes I'll marry you". When I said that Hrithik stood up and took my hand and put the ring to my finger and kissed me on my forehead I just closed my eyes liking the feeling of his lips on my forehead. Then he wrapped his arms around me and pulled me into arms then I also wrapped by hands around his waist and put my head on his chest where I can hear his heart beat. At that I heard all our friends are shouting.

After the late at night everyone came to my home. Yes, it's home because everyday it felt so cold but today here this cold place has been warmed up. I'm very happy today so, I again took my dairy started write on it

"I think it's more than two months since I saw him but from that day on wards, he never leaves my thoughts but seeing him in school I thought its fate that we again meet here. But on my birthday, he made feel special and the day which I marked as a black day on my life by the made

beautiful again. He gave me a family one which always have my back when I'm are in trouble and the one who hold my hand help when I'm scared and the family which never leave me again. But that's not many reasons I feel like home. The only reason is him "My Hrithik" his care, love, gentleness and smile made me come out of the dark. But if anyone asks me why I love him maybe I don't have any reason even if it's there I myself don't know what it is? So, I didn't try to find it because in the depth of my heart I know that I love Hrithik because it's him. He feels like home. My home. He is the reason I dared to let go all my barriers around me. Three years ago, I lost something important to me but after three I got something more precious than that and that is Hrithik. All these years I wanted to let ga all of these but I can't I thought may be time can heal but now I know that "time will never heal any thing it's just teaches us how to bear with the pain but when the right person came into our life then their company is enough to heal everything." And for me that person is Hrithik."

"HE IS MY FAIRYTALE; HE IS MY PRINCE. But for our story it's just a beginning. And I'm ready to walk with him forever and I'm ready face whatever comes in our I'll fight with it if it means to stay by his side forever."

Closing my dairy, I went near the window where I can always watch the moon. While I'm watching a smile is placed on my face and my heart feels clam then I felt his hand wrapped around my waist and placing his chin on my shoulder we stood there like that and I heard him say "You made me happy princess Thank you". Then I turned around and wrapped my arms around his neck keeping my face in in his neck I said "I'm the one who should need to thank you Hrithik fir loving me. I Love You Hrithik". "Love you too princess" saying that he held me tightly in his arms. Then I said "You are my fairy tale Hrithik my only prince". When I said that I saw smile on his face which proves that he's really satisfied with what I said.